One thing became clear. It was now the 24th of May. I had to disappear until the end of the second week in June. Then somehow I had to get in touch with our government people and tell them the facts.

It is the beginning of summer, 1914. The countries of Europe are getting ready for war. Richard Hannay is in London, looking for something interesting to do – and when he meets Franklin P. Scudder, he knows he has found it.

Because Scudder is a spy. The information he has can save a life – and possibly Europe. If Scudder can warn the British government when the time is right, he can stop the biggest war in history. But then someone kills Scudder – and Hannay is next on their list. Suddenly Hannay is running from the murderers and from the police. He must stay alive; he must save his country – but to do that he must understand the secret of the thirty-nine steps . . .

The Thirty-nine Steps is one of the most famous spy stories ever written, and one of several that John Buchan (1875–1940) wrote about the First World War. Buchan knew what he was writing about from his own life, which was full of adventure.

He was born in Scotland and went to Glasgow and Oxford Universities. He loved exciting stories and wrote *The Thirty-nine Steps*, his first spy book, while he was ill in bed. When war began in Europe, in 1914, he went to France to report on it for newspapers, and he also worked for the British government there helping spies.

Buchan wrote over a hundred books in his life, as well as doing other important work: in 1935, the British government made him Governor-General of Canada. People have always loved *The Thirty-nine Steps*. It was made into a film by Alfred Hitchcock in 1935.

OTHER TITLES IN THE SERIES

Level 1
Girl Meets Boy
The Hen and the Bull
The Medal of Brigadier Gerard

Level 2
The Birds
Chocky
Don't Look Now
Emily
The Fox
The Ghost of Genny Castle
Grandad's Eleven
The Lady in the Lake
Money to Burn
Persuasion
The Railway Children
The Room in the Tower and Other
    Ghost Stories
Simply Suspense
Treasure Island
Under the Greenwood Tree

Level 3
Black Beauty
The Black Cat and Other Stories
The Book of Heroic Failures
A Catskill Eagle
The Darling Buds of May
Detective Work
Dubliners
Earthdark
Jane Eyre
King Solomon's Mines
Madame Doubtfire
The Man with Two Shadows and
    Other Ghost Stories
Mrs Dalloway
My Family and Other Animals
Rain Man
The Reluctant Queen
Sherlock Holmes and the Mystery
    of Boscombe Pool
Time Bird
Twice Shy

Level 4
The Boys from Brazil
The Breathing Method
The Danger
The Doll's House and Other Stories
Dracula
Far from the Madding Crowd
Farewell, My Lovely
Glitz
Gone with the Wind, Part 1
Gone with the Wind, Part 2
The House of Stairs
The Locked Room and Other
    Horror Stories
The Mill on the Floss
The Mosquito Coast
The Picture of Dorian Gray
Strangers on a Train
White Fang

Level 5
The Baby Party and Other Stories
The Firm
The Grass is Singing
Jude the Obscure
The Old Jest
The Pelican Brief
Pride and Prejudice
Prime Suspect
A Twist in the Tale
The Warden
Web

Level 6
The Edge
The Long Goodbye
Misery
Mrs Packletide's Tiger and Other
    Stories
The Moonstone
Presumed Innocent
A Tale of Two Cities
The Thorn Birds
Wuthering Heights

The Thirty-nine Steps

JOHN BUCHAN

Level 3

Retold by J. Y. K. Kerr
Series Editor: Derek Strange

PENGUIN BOOKS

PENGUIN BOOKS

Published by the Penguin Group
Penguin Books Ltd, 27 Wrights Lane, London W8 5TZ, England
Penguin Books USA Inc., 375 Hudson Street, New York, New York 10014, USA
Penguin Books Australia Ltd, Ringwood, Victoria, Australia
Penguin Books Canada Ltd, 10 Alcorn Avenue, Toronto, Ontario, Canada M4V 3B2
Penguin Books (NZ) Ltd, 182–190 Wairau Road, Auckland 10, New Zealand

Penguin Books Ltd, Registered Offices: Harmondsworth, Middlesex, England

The Thirty-nine Steps was first published in 1915
Ths adaptation published by Penguin Books 1993
5 7 9 10 8 6 4

Text copyright © J. Y. K. Kerr 1993
Illustrations copyright © David Cuzik 1993
All rights reserved

The moral right of the adapter and of the illustrator has been asserted

Datix International Limited, Bungay, Suffolk
Set in 11/14pt Lasercomp Bembo
Printed in England by Clays Ltd, St Ives plc

To the teacher:

In addition to all the language forms of Levels One and Two, which are used again at this level of the series, the main verb forms and tenses used at Level Three are:

- past continuous verbs, present perfect simple verbs, conditional clauses (using the 'first' or 'open future' conditional), question tags and further common phrasal verbs
- modal verbs: *have (got) to* and *don't have to* (to express obligation), *need to* and *needn't* (to express necessity), *could* and *was able to* (to describe past ability), *could* and *would* (in offers and polite requests for help), and *shall* (for future plans, offers and suggestions).

Also used are:

- relative pronouns: *who*, *that* and *which* (in defining clauses)
- conjunctions: *if* and *since* (for time or reason), *so that* (for purpose or result) and *while*
- indirect speech (questions)
- participle clauses

Specific attention is paid to vocabulary development in the Vocabulary Work exercises at the end of the book. These exercises are aimed at training students to enlarge their vocabulary systematically through intelligent reading and effective use of a dictionary.

To the student:

Dictionary Words:

- As you read this book, you will find that some words are in darker black ink than the others on the page. Look them up in your dictionary, if you do not already know them, or try to guess the meaning of the words first, without a dictionary.

Before you read

1 *The Thirty-nine Steps* is an adventure story. It happens in 1914. Which of these things do you think will be in the story?

a guns and knives

b televison

c a stolen car

d a tea party

e children's games

f policemen

g helicopters

h telephone calls

2 Look at the first picture in this book. Then try to answer these questions.

a Has the man lying on the floor killed himself?

b How did he die?

c Do you think that the other (living) man in the picture killed him?

d What do you think the living man is feeling?

e Do you think that the living man will call the police?

f If the police find the dead man, what things will they probably do?

g What time of day is it in the picture: morning, afternoon or evening?

h We can see *how* the dead man died but can you guess *why* he died? (If you can't guess, read the story and find out!)

Chapter One

THE MAN WHO DIED

It was three o'clock on an afternoon in May and I was feeling very bored. It was three months since I came to London and the amusements of the great city didn't interest me any more. 'Richard Hannay,' I said to myself, 'you are wasting your time here. You must find something more interesting to do.'

This was my first visit to Britain since I was a child. My father took me from Scotland to East Africa at the age of six and I lived there from then on. I liked my **life** as an **engineer** in Buluwayo. I was rich enough to live comfortably; for years I dreamed of nothing but going back to Britain, my homeland. But now I was here at last, nothing seemed as good as I hoped. I was tired of looking at old buildings, tired of the theatre, tired of going to dinner with people who bored me. The real problem was that I had no close friend to go about with. Here I was, thirty-seven years old, with enough money to have a good time, and all alone. I decided that the best thing was to go back to Africa and take up my old life again.

That afternoon I went to see my bankers about some business and on my way home I went into my favourite bar to have a drink and read the evening papers. There was a lot of information about Karolides, the Greek Prime Minister. The **governments** in Berlin and Vienna did not

7

like him much, the newspaper said, but he seemed to me an honest man and a good friend of Britain: an important player in the **political** game that the European Great **Powers** were playing.

About six o'clock I went home, got dressed, had a meal in a restaurant and went to the theatre. As I walked back to my flat in Portland Place, I looked up at the starry night sky and made a promise to myself. 'I'll stay for one more day and if nothing interesting happens, I'll take the next boat to East Africa.'

The flat where I was staying was in a new building with a doorman. It was in a quiet neighbourhood. An old soldier called Paddock came to clean my rooms at eight o'clock every morning and left at seven in the evening, because I always ate out at night.

I was just putting my key in the door when I suddenly saw someone standing next to me. I was surprised. He was a small thin man with a short brown beard and blue eyes. I realized that he was the person living on the top floor; I sometimes met him on the stairs.

'Can I speak to you?' he said. 'Can I come in for a minute?' His voice sounded troubled and his hand was pressing my arm.

I opened the door and showed him in. Immediately he ran through to the bedroom, looked all round it and ran back again. 'Is the door locked?' he asked, looking very worried. He made quite sure that it was and then said: 'I'm sorry about this. I've thought about talking to you all this week, since things began to get difficult. Will you do something for me?'

'I'll listen to you,' I said. 'I can't promise more than that.'

8

He helped himself to a strong drink and drank it down. 'Forgive me,' he said. 'I feel a bit unsure of myself tonight. You see, at this moment I am a dead man.'

I sat down in an armchair and lit my pipe. 'What does it feel like?' I asked. I was almost sure by now that he was crazy.

He smiled. 'No, I'm not mad — yet,' he said. 'I've watched you for several days now and I think you have a clear head and an honest heart. I'm going to tell you some of my secrets. I'm in deep trouble and I badly need your help. Will you help me?'

'Go on,' I said, 'and then I'll tell you.'

'I'm an American', he said, 'from Kentucky; and when I finished my studies, I decided to see the world. I did some writing for a Chicago newspaper and spent a year or two in South-Eastern Europe. I'm good at languages and I got to know a lot of important people in those countries. I got mixed up in politics, at first because it interested me. Later, it was impossible to pull out. I couldn't get free.'

He then told me about a dangerous political movement and the rich businessmen who hoped to make money out of it. He talked a lot about the Balkan War, about how some well-known people disappeared and how some countries got power over others. It seemed that this secret political group was trying to turn Russia and Germany against each other. (They thought that if there was enough political confusion they could take power and change the world.) What they wanted was to see all Europe at war. 'Do you know the name Constantine Karolides?' he said suddenly.

This made me sit up: the man the newspapers were writing about.

'Well, he knows what's going on. He's an honest man and able to put a stop to their plans. For the last twelve months their men have followed Karolides but he has very good bodyguards. Now I've found out how they plan to kill him; and to know that **fact** is deadly dangerous. That's why I'm as good as dead. On the 14th of June Karolides will be in London for a meeting with the British government. And that's when they're going to kill him.'

'Why don't you warn him?' I said.

'But don't you see that he's the only person that can straighten out Europe's political problems?' he answered.

'Why not warn the British government then?'

'That's no good either,' he said. 'Our enemies are too clever. They want Karolides killed while the eyes of the world are on him. An Austrian will do the killing and that will turn everyone against Vienna and Berlin. But there's one person who can stop it all from happening and that's me – Franklin P. Scudder.'

'How did you find out about all this?' I asked.

'I first heard about it in Austria and I learned the final facts ten days ago in Paris. I've changed my name, my hair, my beard and my clothes several times since then to make sure that no one could follow me. Until yesterday I was feeling perfectly happy but then . . .'

He helped himself to another Scotch.

'Then I saw a man standing in the street outside. I thought I knew him . . . He came in and spoke to the doorman. And when I came back from my walk last night, I found a card in my letter box. On it was the name of the man I fear most in the whole world.'

'So what did you do next?'

'I planned my own death. I bought a dead body – it's

10

always possible to do that in a city like London – and I brought it back in a big wooden box. It was about my size. I dressed it in the clothes I was wearing, put it in my bed and shot part of the face away, so that when people find it, they'll think it's me. I left my gun next to the body. I changed my own clothes, too, but didn't dare go into the street. It was much too dangerous. I've stayed inside the building all day, waiting to speak to you. So now you know as much as I do about this whole business.'

I could see that he was terribly frightened but still just able to control himself. 'Give me your key,' I said. 'I want to have a look at this dead body. I have to make sure that your story is true.'

He shook his head sadly. 'I haven't got it. I left it in the room. If the key is missing, they'll know that something is wrong. Believe me, just for tonight, and tomorrow you'll hear all you want to know about the dead man upstairs.'

I thought for a minute. 'Right. I'll have to believe you. I'll lock you in this room, just to make sure. You seem honest enough to me but if you're not, I must warn you that I have my own gun and I know how to use it.'

'Thank you, sir!' he said warmly. 'I don't know your name but you're a really kind man. Can I borrow something to shave with?'

I took him into the bedroom and left him there. After half an hour he came out looking quite different. His face was brown, his hair was cut shorter, and he looked like a British **gentleman** just back from India.

'How you've changed, Mr Scudder!' I cried.

'Not Mr Scudder,' he answered. 'I'm Captain Theophilus Digby, serving in the Indian army. Kindly remember that, sir.'

11

I made him a bed in the sitting-room and then went to mine, feeling more alive than at any time in the past month. In this unexciting city, it seemed that exciting things did sometimes happen.

I woke up next morning with my cleaner knocking hard on the sitting-room door. 'Stop that noise, Paddock,' I told him. 'A friend of mine, Captain ... (I couldn't remember his name) is sleeping in there. Get breakfast for two ready and then come and speak to me.'

I told Paddock that my friend was tired out and needed a good long rest from his work; and to escape from phone calls and visitors. When Scudder came in, looking just like a British army gentleman, he played his part beautifully, talking to Paddock about army life and to me about a number of friends I didn't know I had. I left him with the newspaper and a box of cigars and went off to see my bankers again. When I got back, the doorman was full of important news.

'A bad business here this morning, sir. The gentleman in Number 15 has shot himself. They've just taken him away. The police are up there now.'

I went up to Number 15 and asked the police some stupid questions. They soon told me to leave. I spoke to Scudder's cleaning man but I could see that he didn't think that there was anything odd. Everyone believed that Scudder killed himself.

I told Scudder all this and he was deeply interested. For the first two days that he stayed with me in the back room, he was very calm. He read and smoked and wrote things in a notebook. But by the third day I could see that he was getting restless. He made a list of the days until June 14th and wrote notes in **code** next to them. He spent a lot of time thinking and sometimes looked downhearted. He asked me again and again if Paddock was honest and able to keep his mouth shut. Once or twice he spoke to me quite angrily and then said that he was sorry. I understood. He had a very difficult job to do. He was not worrying about himself but about his plans to save Karolides' life. One night he became very serious.

'Listen, Hannay,' he said. 'I think I must tell you more about this business. If they get me, I want someone to be able to continue the fight.' And he began to give me many more facts.

I must say that I wasn't listening very carefully. I was really more interested in his adventures than in all his political information. Karolides and the rest of them were not my business, I thought, and I immediately forgot many of the things he told me. I remember that he explained that there was no danger to Karolides until he arrived in London. The danger then was from high-up people – a danger that no one was ready for. He spoke of a woman – Julia Czechenyi – who had something to do with the murder plan. She was the key, he said, the person who was going to get Karolides away from his bodyguards. He talked, too, about a Black Stone and a man who spoke with a lisp* and he repeatedly pointed to the person he was most afraid of – an old man with a young voice, who had strange **eyelids** that sometimes came down over his eyes.

He also spoke a lot about dying. His thoughts were all about finishing his work: clearly, he didn't care about saving his life.

'Dying, I guess, is just like going to sleep when you're

---

* A way of speaking in which the 's' sound becomes 'th'.

My friend Scudder was lying on his back on the floor. There was a long knife right through his heart.

really tired', he said. 'Then you wake up to find a summer day like the ones I remember as a boy in Kentucky.'

Next day he seemed a lot happier and spent much of his time reading. I went out to have supper with another engineer I knew and came back about half past ten, in time for a talk before bedtime. The lights were all off when I went into the flat and I found that strange. I thought Scudder was perhaps already in bed. Then I saw something which made me jump with **fear**. My friend Scudder was lying on his back on the floor. There was a long knife right through his heart.

Chapter Two

THE MILKMAN GOES OFF ON HIS TRAVELS

I sat down in an armchair and felt very sick. His poor white face seemed to be watching me and I couldn't look at it, so I covered it with a kitchen towel. I needed a strong drink. I knew what dead men looked like from the war in South Africa but this was different. Slowly I got control of myself, helped by the drink. I looked at my watch: it was half past ten.

I had a sudden idea, and looked all over the flat very carefully. There was nobody there. I shut all the windows and locked the door. I was beginning to think more clearly now. There was no hurry, because if the murderer didn't come back I had until six o'clock in the morning to make my plans.

It was clear that I was in deep trouble. I knew that

Scudder's story was true: that was why he was now dead. His enemies wanted to make sure of his silence and this was the best way. But it was four days since he moved into my rooms and his enemies must realize that I knew a lot about him. That meant that I was the next on their list. Perhaps that night, or the next day, or the day after . . . They were sure to get me sooner or later.

Suddenly I thought of another problem. 'If I go and call the police,' I said to myself, 'how am I going to explain why Scudder died in my flat?' When he first arrived, I lied to Paddock about who he was. 'If I tell the police the true facts, they're just going to laugh at me,' I thought. They were sure to think that I was the murderer. Perhaps that was just what Scudder's enemies were hoping for: to have me in prison until after June 14th. 'And if I do tell the story, then Karolides will stay in Greece, which is just what they want. Now that Scudder is dead, it's up to me to continue his work.'

After an hour or two of thinking, one thing became clear. It was now the 24th of May. I had to disappear until the end of the second week in June. Then somehow I had to get in touch with our government people and tell them the facts that Scudder told me. 'I only hope that they'll believe me,' I thought, as I began to look through Scudder's pockets. I wanted his little black notebook but it wasn't there. I guessed that the murderer probably took it. Then I noticed that the papers in my desk — and other things in the flat — were out of place. But I still couldn't find the book: it must already be in enemy hands.

I got out a map of Britain. My idea was to go to some wild, far-away part of the country. I thought of Scotland. My family came from there and I could easily pretend to

16

be an ordinary Scotsman. I decided on Galloway as the best place to go. It was the nearest wild part, with not many people living there. I looked up the train times and saw that a train left Saint Pancras station at seven ten, taking me to any Galloway station by late afternoon. But how was I to get to Saint Pancras? Scudder's killers were sure to be watching the building from the street. Then I had another bright idea and went to bed for just two hours of troubled sleep.

I got up at four and saw the light of a fine summer morning growing stronger. For a minute I thought what I was planning to do was crazy: I was not really afraid, I just felt that I was getting deeper into trouble. I put on a warm shirt, an old woollen suit and a pair of strong boots, and I put a clean shirt, an old hat, some handkerchiefs and a toothbrush in my pocket. I had plenty of money in the flat and I now put fifty pounds in my back pocket. Then I had a bath and a shave and changed the shape of my moustache.

Then came my next move. Paddock usually arrived at half past seven and he had a key. But at twenty minutes to seven the milkman usually came, making a great noise with his milk bottles and leaving some bottles outside my door. He was a youngish man, about my size, with a small moustache and a long white coat. He didn't know it but he was going to help me.

I had a Scotch and some dry bread for breakfast. By this time it was nearly six o'clock. I put a pipe in my pocket and went to the tin where I kept my **tobacco**. I put my hand inside and my fingers touched something hard: Scudder's little notebook! It, too, went into my pocket.

I took the towel off Scudder's face and said goodbye.

17

'Send me some luck, my friend,' I said, and went to wait by the front door.

Today of all days the milkman was late. At a quarter to seven I heard him coming, so I opened the front door, making him jump. 'Come in for a minute,' I said. 'I want to ask you something. Can I borrow your hat and coat for ten minutes? I'll give you a pound.'

He seemed a little surprised but he said yes. I told him to wait until I came back.

'All right, sir,' he said. 'I like a bit of sport.'

I put on his flat blue hat and white coat, picked up his bottles and went noisily down the stairs. I saw a policeman in the street and another man with his eyes on the front door. I crossed the street, turned into the first side street and dropped the hat, coat and bottles in a dark doorway. Just then I heard a church clock telling me it was already seven.

There was not a second to lose. As soon as I got to Euston Road, I started running. At Saint Pancras I had no time to get a ticket, in fact I didn't really know where I was going. I saw the train already beginning to move and jumped onto it just in time.

Three minutes later, an angry guard was writing out a ticket for me to Newton Stewart, a place-name I suddenly remembered; and I then found somewhere to sit between a sailor and a fat woman with a child. The woman was angry with the guard, who wanted her to buy a ticket for her little girl. The sad-looking sailor was agreeing with her. As the train ate up the miles between London and Scotland, I began to feel like a new person. How strange that only a week ago I was thinking that life in this country was boring!

The milkman seemed a little surprised but he said yes.
'All right, sir,' he said. 'I like a bit of sport.'

Chapter Three

THE HOTEL-KEEPER WHO LOVED BOOKS

As I sat in the train travelling north, I got out Scudder's little black book. It was full of numbers and clearly this was some kind of code where the numbers stood for letters. The problem was that I didn't have the key to the code. I tried for hours but I could get no meaning out of it. I fell asleep and woke up at Dumfries, just in time to get out and catch the slow train to Galloway. At the station, I looked at myself in a mirror: with my brown face and my old woollen suit, I looked just like one of the crowd of hill farmers getting onto the train. I sat with a group of them, listening to their talk of sheep prices at the market. Finally, about five o'clock, they all got out and I was alone. I got out at the next stop, where the station man was busy in his vegetable garden and a child of about ten took my ticket. In front of me was a white road, cutting across the open hills.

It was a beautiful late spring evening and the air was perfectly clear. I felt as happy as a boy, instead of like a man wanted by the police. I walked for some time but I was beginning to feel hungry – it was hours since I ate anything. Soon I came to a little house, with water running past it. A country woman was standing by the door and I asked if I could stay the night.

'You're welcome to a bed under the roof,' she said and soon brought me a meal of eggs and sausages and bread and milk. She and her husband were good people: they asked me no questions and by ten o'clock I was falling asleep and very ready for that bed.

20

The next day they would not agree to take any money and after a good breakfast I left, walking back towards the south. My idea was to get to a railway station one or two stops after the place where I got off the train the day before. The police were sure to think that I was moving west, hoping to get away by sea. I was probably safe for a few more hours, if I was lucky.

The weather was still fine and young sheep and their mothers covered the green hillsides. I felt healthy and full of hope. The hill I was on went down to a little river and I could see the smoke of a train a mile away and coming nearer.

The station, when I got there, was perfect for what I wanted, without any road to or from it. I hid until the train arrived and then bought a ticket for Dumfries. I found a place next to a drunk old man and his sheepdog. The man was asleep, with a morning newspaper beside him. I started reading it. There was a lot about the 'Portland Place murder' in it. The police at first **arrested** the milkman but now he was free again. The paper said that the police believed the real criminal to be somewhere in the north. There was nothing in the paper about Karolides or the things that interested Scudder.

The train stopped at the station where I began yesterday evening's walk. I saw three men, police probably, questioning the station man, so I sat well back in the shadows. Someone was pointing to the white road that went from the station across the hills.

The train moved on and then I had some luck. It stopped by a bridge over a river in the middle of the country. No one was watching, so I opened the door and dropped down among some thick trees beside the railway

21

line. But the dog thought I was stealing the man's belongings and followed me, making a terrible noise and trying to bite me. The old man woke up and stood shouting at the train door; he probably believed that I was trying to kill myself.

Soon the guard and some passengers came along and began looking towards the place where I was hiding. I moved carefully away on my hands and knees and, when I looked back some minutes later, I saw that the train was moving off again.

I was now in a wide half-circle of open grassland, with a few small trees and high hills to the north. I could not see or hear a single person, just the sound of water and the calling of birds. But for the first time I felt I was a wanted man. It was not the police I was afraid of, but Scudder's killers. They wanted to see me dead like Scudder – I knew that – and they were very clever.

I began to run and didn't stop until I got to the top of a hill high above the railway and the small brown river. From here I could see the land for miles around: nothing moved. To the east, there were shallow green valleys, forests and what looked like roads. But when I looked up at the blue sky, I saw something that made me cold with fear.

Low down in the south a small aeroplane was climbing into the sky. I knew immediately that it was looking for me and that it didn't belong to the police. For an hour or two I watched it flying low over the hilltops and then in narrow circles over the valley where I got off the train. At last it turned and flew away back to the south. I didn't like this place where I was so easy to see from the air, so I decided to move on. I went towards the green country to

The old man stood shouting at the train door; he probably believed that I was trying to kill myself.

the east, where I knew there were trees and stone houses and places to hide.

About six in the evening I came to a road with one house standing alone. In front of it was a young man reading a book.

'Is this place a hotel?' I asked.

'It is,' he answered, 'and it's mine. Would you like to stay the night?'

'You're young to be a hotel-keeper,' I said.

'My father died a year ago and left me the business. I must say it isn't what I really wanted to do.'

'Which was?'

'I want to write books,' the young man said. 'I want to see the world, have lots of adventures and write about them.'

'Adventures can happen anywhere,' I said. 'I'll tell you mine, and in a month from now you can turn them into a book.' We sat outside on that soft May evening and I told him a wonderful story: how a bunch of gangsters killed my best friend and were now following me. It began in Africa and ended with the murder in Portland Place. He believed every word.

'You'll be perfectly safe here,' he said. As we went into the house, I heard the sound of the plane again: it was coming back.

I had a good meal and a good sleep. Next morning I sent him off on his bicycle to get the morning newspaper, telling him to look out for strangers.

He came back at midday. There was more about the murder but also a long piece about Karolides and political problems in the Balkan countries. I sat down to study Scudder's notebook again. What was the key to the code?

Without that, I felt helpless. Suddenly I remembered the name Julia Czechenyi. Scudder once said that she was the 'key' to the Karolides business. It worked. 'Julia' gave me the numbers for the letters A, E, I, O and U. A was J, the tenth letter and X in Scudder's code; E was U = XXI, and so on. 'Czechenyi' gave me most of the other letters.

Soon, full of excitement, I was reading page after page. I looked out of the window and saw a big car coming towards the hotel. Two men got out, wearing raincoats. Ten minutes later the hotel-keeper came noiselessly in, looking very worried. 'There are two men looking for you,' he said in a low voice. 'They said they were hoping to meet you here. They described you very well. I told them you were here last night and that you left very early this morning. They were far from pleased!'

He told me that one was thin with dark hair and eyes and the other was always smiling and spoke with a lisp. Neither was foreign: he was sure about that.

I wrote a page in German, to look like part of a letter, with these words:

'. . . Black Stone. Scudder knew but he could do nothing for two weeks. I don't think I can do any good now, because Karolides is still not sure about his plans. But if Mr T. agrees, I will do the best I . . .'

'Take this downstairs and say you found it in my bedroom,' I said. 'Ask them to give it back to me when they find me.'

Three minutes later I heard the car starting up and I was just able to get a look at the two men as they left.

The hotel-keeper was really enjoying himself. 'The dark one went white when he read your note,' he said, 'and the fat one looked very angry. They left in a great hurry.'

25

'Take this downstairs and say you found it in my bedroom.'

'This is what I want you to do now,' I said. 'Go to Newton Stewart and tell the police there about the two men. Say that you think they had a hand in the London murder. They'll be back here tomorrow, you can be sure, so tell the police to get here early.'

I did some more work on Scudder's notes for the rest of the day and we had supper together that evening. I told him lots more stories about Africa. Then I stayed up late and finished Scudder's book.

Next morning three policemen arrived by car. Soon a second car appeared, coming towards the hotel, but it stopped by some trees about two hundred yards away. Soon I heard the two men outside. At first I thought of waiting to see what happened. Then I had a better idea. I

26

wrote a few lines of thanks to my young friend and climbed quietly out of the window into the back garden. I made my way to the car, jumped in and drove away.

A turn in the road soon hid me from the hotel, but I seemed to hear the sound of angry voices carried by the wind as I made my escape.

Chapter Four

THE FOOLISH POLITICIAN

I drove like the wind that shining May morning, always watching both behind me and in front. But I was also thinking hard about what was in Scudder's notebook. A lot of what he first told me was not really true: the real facts were much worse. A dangerous group of people were planning a war, and Karolides' murder on the 14th of June was to be the way it started. 'Austria will then move into the Balkans,' I thought, 'and that will make Russia angry. Then Germany will take Austria's side.' But Germany was really planning to make war on Britain, and none of us here seemed to realize that. The danger was very great. On June 15th a secret meeting between France and Britain was to take place in London, and the Germans – that is, the Black Stone – were planning something to do with that meeting. Somehow they were going to get hold of our secret **defence** plans, and make use of them as soon as the war began. Five or six times in the notebook came the words 'the thirty-nine steps'. I had no idea what they meant.

To think that here in this sleepy part of Scotland I now knew all this! I first thought of writing to the Government

27

but I soon realized that this was useless. I had to talk to somebody important face to face. But who? And how? I drove on, through pretty little villages, past quiet rivers. At midday I came to a long village street. A policeman was standing outside the post office with a paper in his hand. He tried to make me stop but I drove straight past him and took a road up into the hills.

Suddenly I saw another car coming out of a side road, where there was a big house standing in parkland. 'We're going to crash!' I thought, but just in time I drove off the road, and my car broke through some young trees by the roadside. It fell down fifty feet into a river, with a terrible noise of breaking glass and metal against stone. But luck was still with me. As the car fell, its door suddenly opened, I fell out to one side, and my body hit a tree. The car crashed down into the river below me. Badly shaken, I climbed down from the tree to the ground.

A tall young man in a leather driving coat ran over to me. 'My dear sir, are you hurt?' he asked in a frightened voice.

'No, I'm all right,' I told him.

'Then come back to my house and lie down for a bit.'

He put me into his car and drove to a comfortable-looking house standing among trees. He showed me to a bedroom and took out some of his suits because my clothes were cut to pieces.

'Were your bags in the car?' he asked.

'No, this is all I have,' I said, taking out my toothbrush. 'In Africa, where I come from, we travel light.'

'You're from Africa!' he cried. 'You're just the man I need! Do you believe in the Free Market?'

'Of course,' I answered, without any idea what he meant.

The car fell into the river with a terrible noise. As the car fell, its door suddenly opened, I fell out to one side, and my body hit a tree.

'Will you come with me to a political meeting then?' he asked. 'We must leave in five minutes.'

He gave me a coffee and some cold meat and hurried me away to his car. As he drove, I told him that I was a tourist and that my name was Twisdon. He explained that the speaker for his meeting was ill. 'Can you take his place and give a talk on the Free Market?' he asked.

'I don't know much about politics,' I answered, 'but I can tell them a bit about Australia.' His face shone with happiness. He began telling me about himself. He was a sportsman, loved shooting and fishing and horses, and he wanted to become a politician. I soon realized that he wasn't very intelligent but that he had a heart of gold.

Just then we saw a light moving in the middle of the roadway and the car slowed down. A village policeman's face appeared at the window. My blood turned cold. 'Pardon, Sir Harry, we've been told to watch out for a car that looks like yours. Sorry to trouble you.' And we drove on.

When we got to the meeting and he stood up to speak, my ideas about Sir Harry seemed to be right. He was a hopeless speaker, always stopping and starting again, repeating himself endlessly, dropping his notes. When they called on me to speak, I just told them everything I knew about Australia, hoping that none of the listeners came from there. Everyone seemed to think I was a great speaker, most of all my new friend.

'You must stay for a few days,' he said, as we drove home. 'The fishing is quite good round here, you know.'

After a big hot supper, we sat by the fire and I decided to talk to him seriously. I told him the true story: Scudder, the milkman, the notebook, my adventures in Galloway, the danger of a war with Germany. He listened in silence to every word. Finally he said 'I believe you. What can I do to help?'

'You told me you had an uncle in the Government,' I said. 'I want you to write him a letter. I must see him before the 14th of June, which is when they plan to kill Karolides.'

'No, I can do better than that,' he said. 'My godfather is Sir Walter Bullivant. He's a very important man in the Foreign Office. I'll write to him. He lives at Artinswell in Wiltshire.'

'Tell him that a man called Twisdon (my new name) wants to see him on very important secret business. He will know me by the words 'Black Stone' and if he hears someone **whistling** a Scottish song.'

'Right,' said Sir Harry. 'Can I do anything more?'

'Let me borrow a suit of clothes and a map of this part of the country. If the police come looking for me, show them the car in the river. If the other men appear, tell them I took a train back south.'

I slept until two o'clock in the morning, as we agreed, and then he woke me up. He gave me a bicycle and showed me the best road to take. 'Go up on the hills,' he told me. 'You'll be perfectly safe there.'

I thanked him warmly and rode off into the darkness. As it grew light, I found myself high up among the green hills, able to see across country for miles on every side. Here I could surely get early warning of my enemies.

Chapter Five

THE ROADMENDER

It was now about seven o'clock. The smooth green hills around me didn't have a single tree on them and I realized that I was not as safe as I first thought. The unwelcome sound of an aeroplane coming in high from the east, then flying lower in small circles made me drop to the ground but I was sure the pilot noticed me. I saw the other person in the plane looking at me through his field glasses. I pushed the bicycle into a pool of water and started climbing up the hillside. Far below me I could see a road and a car travelling fast. But worse still, down in the valley I noticed a line of men walking slowly up the hills towards me . . . I dropped below the skyline. I couldn't go on that way; I must try the bigger hills to the south. I ran hard and thought I saw one or two more people moving on the hillside above me. There wasn't a hole or a stone anywhere – nowhere for me to hide.

Just then, I saw a narrow road and at the side of it, standing by a little mountain of stones, a roadman. He was a wild-looking man with a week's beard on his face and a big pair of glasses on his nose. He also looked as sick as a dog.

'It's my first day at this job,' he said in a loud voice, 'and all I want is my bed. I was drinking with the boys last night and my head is heavier than these stones here. And my boss is coming round any minute now to see me at work.'

'Does he know what you look like?' I asked, suddenly full of hope.

'Not him,' was the answer. 'He's nearly as new to his job as I am.'

32

'Well off to your bed,' I said. 'I'll take your place.'

'That's a great offer, man,' said the roadmender. 'I'm Sandy Turnbull but my friends call me Ecky, or sometimes Specky, because of these glasses I wear.' He took them off and gave them to me along with his dirty old hat and pipe. I gave him my jacket and tie to carry home. My face and arms, brown from the African sun, looked right, but I dirtied my boots, hands and face to look more like a real roadman.

Specky went off to his little house not far away, and I began breaking and carrying stones as he was doing when I arrived. For a long time no one went past and nothing happened.

Suddenly a young man in a Ford car appeared. Without getting out, he said, 'Are you Alexander Turnbull? Your work's not bad. I'll be along to see you again in a day or two.' Then he drove away. That was how I got through my first test.

A travelling shop passed and sold me some bread; then a farm worker, who asked 'Where's Specky?'

'He's ill in bed,' I answered and went on with my work.

At about midday, a big car came down the hill past me and stopped a hundred yards away. Three people got out. Two of them I already knew: the thin dark one and the fat smiling one. The third was dressed like a small farmer but the eyes in his head were quick and questioning.

'Good morning,' he said. 'That's an easy job you've got.'

I answered slowly, speaking like a Lowland Scot. 'I've had better jobs than this and I've had worse too.'

'Did you see a stranger go past early this morning? On a bicycle or perhaps on foot?' asked the other.

'I got here about seven and since then I've only seen two people from the village until you gentleman came by.'

'I wasn't at work very early,' I answered. 'My daughter was married last night and we were up until late. I got here about seven and since then I've only seen two people from the village until you gentlemen came by.'

One of the men gave me a cigar and they drove on. Some time later they came past me again and waved. Clearly they were being very careful.

At about five o'clock, I decided to go down to Turnbull's house to pick up my things but just then a new car came up the road and stopped a yard or two away. The driver wanted to smoke a cigarette and asked me for matches. I looked up and to my great surprise, realized that I knew this man. He was a young businessman called Marmaduke Jopley, who spent his time making friends with the rich. He was sure to be on his way to stay with some of his rich friends.

'Hello, Jopley,' I said. 'Well met!' He was very surprised.

'Who are you?' he asked.

'Hannay, from East Africa,' I said.

'Good **God**! The murderer!' he cried.

'That's right; and there'll be a second murder if you don't give me your coat this minute; and your hat too.'

He did as he was told, looking terribly afraid. I put on his good thick driving-coat and then his hat. Once again I looked quite different. I got into the car and made him sit next to me. We drove back the way he came until it was dark. Watchers at the roadside knew the car and let it go past without stopping. After dark I turned up into a valley and drove until all the villages and farms were far behind us. I stopped on an empty piece of hillside and gave Jopley back his belongings.

'A thousand thanks,' I said. 'You're more useful than I thought. Now go and find the police.'

I sat on the hillside in the darkness, watching his car lights get smaller, and thought about myself: I was not a murderer but I was already a liar and a car thief.

Chapter Six

THE MAN WITH NO HAIR

I lay on the hillside all night behind a big stone. I felt very cold because my coat was still with Turnbull, and in it was my watch, my tobacco and Scudder's notebook. All I had with me was some money and the bread bought from the travelling shop that morning. I ate half of the bread but I was still terribly hungry. I dreamed of Paddock's breakfast of sausages and eggs, and dinners at good restaurants. I woke as it was getting light, feeling very tired. I looked out down the valley and what I saw made me put on my boots in a hurry. There were men below, moving up the hill, looking behind every stone.

I ran for half a mile behind the skyline, then showed myself for a minute. The men saw me and I heard their cries. I then ran back behind the hill nearly to my sleeping place. The men ran up the hill past me, going the wrong way. I had a start of about twenty minutes but that was not much. I ran and ran until at last I came to quite a big farmhouse. I moved on my stomach across some open ground, ran again under the cover of some trees and finally got into the garden of the old farm. I looked up to find an old gentleman quietly watching me from a window. I went in through a glass door and found myself in a pleasant room full of books. Sitting at a desk in the middle of the room was the kind-looking old gentleman, with glasses on the end of his nose and a hairless head as shiny as a bottle. He didn't move but looked up at me, waiting for me to speak.

I really didn't know what to say, so I said nothing.

'You seem in a great hurry, my friend,' said the old man slowly. He looked out of the window and noticed the men on the hillside. 'Ah, I see. You're running away. Well, we can find out why later. I don't want the police in here. Go into my library, then take the door on the left and close it behind you. You will be quite safe there.'

I did as he told me and found myself in a small dark room with a strange smell. I was safe but I felt uneasy. There was something odd about the old gentleman that made me feel almost afraid. He seemed to show no surprise, in some way to know that I was coming. All I could do was wait.

At last there was a sound and the door opened. I came out into the sunlight to find the old man sitting in an armchair, looking at me with questioning eyes. His hand rested on the table in front of him and the fingers moved like someone playing the **piano**. He waited for me to speak.

'Have they gone?' I asked.

'They have. I told them that I saw you crossing the hill. I didn't want the police to come between us. This is a lucky day for you, Mr Richard Hannay.'

As he spoke, his eyelids seemed to come down and cover his eyes. At once I remembered Scudder's words about the man he feared most in the world: 'the man with the strange eyelids'. Suddenly I saw that I was anything but safe; instead, I was in the hands of my enemies.

37

My first thought was to run; but as I turned, I saw two men with guns standing behind me.

I thought fast. 'I don't know what you're talking about. Who's Richard Hannay? My name's Ainslie.'

'Of course,' said the old man. 'I'm sure you have many names.' His fingers still moved like a piano-player's.

I tried my best to look angry. 'I know you're going to give me up to the police. It was a mistake to go near that man's car. Here, take the money back!' And I threw four pounds on the table.

He opened his eyes a little. 'Oh no, we shall not give you up. We have a little business to finish with you first. You're very clever, Mr Hannay, but not quite clever enough!'

'Oh, give it a rest!' I cried. 'I've had no luck since I got off the boat in Leith. Yes, I did steal four pounds from that car; but I was hungry and I needed to eat. Now the police have chased me all over these hills. It's not right, I tell you. But I've had enough.'

He was beginning to be less sure of me.

'Give me a bite to eat, sir, just a mouthful of food and I'll tell you the story from start to finish.'

He believed this, I think, because one of the men brought me some cold meat and a glass of beer. I ate like a pig – or like Ned Ainslie, the sailor I was pretending to be.

I told them how I was coming to visit my brother in Wigton, how I found the crashed car with the money inside, how a woman in a bread shop thought there was something odd about me and sent for the police, and about the chase over the hills.

Clearly the old man half-believed my story but he said, 'Of course I'm not going to let you go. We'll soon know

I tried my best to look angry. 'Here, take the money back.'
And I threw four pounds on the table.

if you really are Ainslie, as you say. If you're not, then I fear your time is up.'

He turned to one of his men, speaking in German. 'I want the car in five minutes,' he said. 'There will be three people for lunch.'

Then he turned back to me, his eyes as cold as a snake's. My heart stopped but I put on a sickly smile.

'Lock him in the darkroom until I return,' he said. His men took me out of the room with a gun at each ear.

♦

Alone in that empty darkroom, I had plenty of time to think.

'The old man has gone off in the car to pick up the other two,' I thought. 'They'll remember me, because I'm still dressed as a roadman. In an hour or two they'll be back, and then it will all be over. A shot in the back of the head is what I'll get.'

The only thing which kept me going was that I was so angry: about Scudder, about Karolides, about falling like this into my enemies' hands. I started to look carefully round the room and found a locked cupboard. I pulled hard at the door for some minutes and finally the lock broke. There was that strange smell again: inside were bags, boxes and an electric **torch**. I used the torch to look inside the boxes and, to my great surprise, I found that one of the boxes held **explosives** – everything I needed to make a bomb, in fact. As an engineer, I often used explosives in my work. Then I had a daring idea. It was very dangerous but it was my last hope. Being so angry helped me to do it. I made the thing very slowly and carefully, lit a match, stood well back and – a bright yellow light lit up

40

the room for a second, followed by an explosion to end all explosions. I don't remember what happened next.

I woke up lying in the back garden, with clouds of thick yellow smoke all round me. I felt very sick but pushed myself to a place with running water and put my head into it. The coldness brought me back to life. Then I got as far as an old outbuilding and lay there to rest. Far away I could hear confused shouts and cries. My shoulder was hurting terribly but I realized I could not stay where I was for long: I must find a safer place. Behind the outhouse was a big leafy tree. Climbing up it was one of the hardest things I ever did but I got there somehow. For hours I lay up there more dead than alive, while the men from the house went looking for me everywhere. From where I lay, I could see them, all five now carrying guns. It was hot there under the leaves and I became terribly thirsty: the sound of running water below me just made it worse.

After some hours the car drove away and I also saw a man on a horse crossing and recrossing the hillside. But I saw another thing that surprised me much more. Behind some trees not far from the house there was a secret airfield and, as it got dark, I heard and then saw the aeroplane coming back.

Now it was time to move. I got down from my hiding-place and moved on my stomach until I was well away from the house. Over the hill, I was in open grassland again. I ran for ten minutes and finally stopped by a pool of clear water, where I drank and drank. But I didn't stop going until the house and the airfield were a good ten miles behind me.

41

Chapter Seven

THE WISE FISHERMAN

I still felt very sick and had a terrible headache but I knew I had to get back to Turnbull's house, where my other clothes and Scudder's notebook were waiting. After that, my plan was to go south and find the man in the Foreign Office, Sir Walter Bullivant. It was a wonderful starry night and I still had Sir Harry's map. Turnbull's house was about eighteen miles away and I knew I could only travel by night.

Dog-tired, I started off and at daybreak I again found a small stone-built house, where a kind woman took me in and gave me a meal and an old sheepskin coat. This was a piece of luck, because it began to rain heavily. I spent that day resting under a little bridge but my hurt shoulder kept me awake most of the time. After dark I started off again, twice losing my way. I was feeling light-headed by now, and my legs did not do what I told them any more.

The next morning I finally got to Turnbull's house, more dead than alive. Mr Turnbull opened the door, dressed in a clean black suit with the Good Book* in his hand. I had no idea what day it was, but clearly it was Sunday and he was going to church.

'Have you got my glasses?' was the first thing he said. I took them out of my pocket. Then I fell into a chair and Turnbull put me to bed. I was ill for the next ten days, while that good man nursed me. When I was better, he gave me back my belongings. He told me that a number

---

* The Bible.

42

of people were looking for me but he asked no questions. He didn't want to take any money from me but in the end, with difficulty, I made him take five pounds. A friend of his drove me to the station and I caught the night train south.

About eight o'clock the following evening – the 13th of June – a Scots farm worker in a dirty old sheepskin coat got off a train at Artinswell station in Wiltshire. I didn't dare to ask anyone the way, so I started walking. Soon I came to a bridge across a little river. It was so restful there that I started whistling to myself: 'Annie Laurie', an old Scottish song. A fisherman, hearing the song, came up from the waterside. He was a big man, wearing old clothes and a sun hat but with a kind, intelligent face.

'A great day for fishing,' he said, 'but it's getting too late to catch any more. Look at that big one just by the bank.'

'I can't see him,' I said. 'Oh yes! About four pounds, don't you think? At first I thought he was just a Black Stone.'

The fisherman looked at me closely. 'You're Mr Twisdon, aren't you? Harry's friend.'

'No,' I said. 'I mean yes.' For a second I forgot who I was pretending to be.

The fisherman laughed. 'Come home with me, then,' he said. We made our way to a pretty riverside house with a garden full of flowers. In a bedroom I found a full change of clothes: shirts, ties, shoes and a well-cut suit. A hot bath was already running for me and shaving things were lying near the bath.

An hour later, bathed, shaved and well-dressed, I was sitting at Sir Walter's supper-table, talking about fishing and my sporting life in Africa. After coffee, I told him my

'A great day for fishing,' he said, 'but it's getting too late to catch any more. Look at that big one just by the bank.'

story: about Scudder's murder, Sir Harry, the chase over the hills in Scotland and the famous notebook.

'Have you got it here?' Sir Walter asked.

I took it out of my pocket and gave it to him but said nothing about the notes inside.

Bullivant was specially interested in the men who took me prisoner and I had to describe each of them fully to him.

'Well, you needn't worry any more about the police,' he said. 'You see, Scudder wrote to me just before he died. He told me he was with a good friend and promised to write again before the 14th of June. We found out more about you, Mr Hannay, and when Harry's letter arrived, I was able to guess the rest.'

He now turned to the notebook. I explained the code and he understood it immediately. As he read, his face became more and more serious. When he finished reading, we sat in silence for some minutes.

'I don't fully understand it,' he said at last. 'But he's right about the secret meeting with the French on the 15th. How did he find that out? It was top secret information. But all this business about the Black Stone is just not sensible. And he's quite wrong about the plan to kill Karolides. No one wants that. I don't believe that part of the story. But something very unpleasant *is* going on and sadly what he found out has cost him his life. All this is very serious but it's not as dangerous as he thought it was.'

Just then his housekeeper came into the room. 'A telephone call from London, Sir Walter: for you personally. It's very important, they said.'

Sir Walter went off to the telephone. When he came back, his face was white with worry. 'I'm afraid Scudder

45

was quite right,' he said. 'Someone shot Karolides dead in London this evening, a few minutes after seven.'

Chapter Eight

THE COMING OF THE BLACK STONE

Over breakfast next morning Sir Walter told me that the meeting with the French defence chief, Royer, was going to be a day early – that evening, in fact. He was still unhappy about the fact that Scudder, and perhaps others, knew about this meeting, which was meant to be top secret. 'Royer will have supper with my boss,' Bullivant explained. 'Then he'll come to my house at Queen Anne's Gate. There, four other people will join us: the Navy chief Lord Alloa, Whittaker, also from the Navy, Sir Arthur Drew from Defence and General Winstanley. The Navy will bring our defence plans, and we'll show them to Royer at the meeting. Of course Royer will have special guards for the whole time that he is in this country. And Alloa has a bodyguard too, until the meeting is over. By the way, can you drive? Good, then I want you to be my driver for today, if you agree. Clearly you're a useful man to have around.'

I was happy that there was still a part for me to play and I drove Sir Walter up to London, arriving at his house in Queen Anne's Gate by half past eleven.

He then took me round to the police building at Scotland Yard, where I met MacGillivray, Head of Crime. 'Here's Mr Richard Hannay, the Portland Place murderer!' Bullivant said with a smile. MacGillivray smiled back.

46

'We were very interested in you for some time,' he said.

'Oh, he has more to tell you,' Sir Walter said, 'but that must wait for twenty-four hours. You'll find what he has to say just as interesting, I promise you. We may need your help soon, MacGillivray, with a different problem. I'll let you know.'

As we left, he turned to me. 'Come and see me tomorrow, Hannay. Of course you mustn't say a word about all this. Off you go and enjoy yourself.'

But I felt strangely restless. At last I was a free man but I had nothing special to do now. I had lunch at the Savoy Hotel and took a long walk through the streets of London. But I felt left out, useless: others were busy defending British interests now, not me. And the Black Stone was still working away there, somewhere in the darkness. I knew all about the danger, but what could I do?

After dinner, I decided to go to Queen Anne's Gate. As I was walking along Jermyn Street, a group of young men in evening dress came towards me. One of them was Marmaduke Jopley. He saw me and stopped, surprised.

'By God, it's Hannay, the Portland Place murderer!' he cried. 'Come on, boys, let's get him!'

They tried to hold me back and I hit Jopley hard in the face, knocking him over. A policeman arrived and, as he moved in to arrest me, I broke free but with five or six young men chasing after me. I ran like the wind across St James's Park to Sir Walter's house and knocked repeatedly at the door.

The man who opened it explained that Sir Walter was in a meeting and I must wait until it ended. I told him that some people were following me and asked him to send away any policemen who called.

47

I sat on a chair just inside the entrance, waiting for Bullivant. The police soon appeared and the man told them that I was not in the house. But the next caller was none other than the Navy Chief, Lord Alloa, whose face I knew well from the newspapers, with its well-cut grey beard, long nose and intelligent blue eyes. He went into the meeting and the door shut behind him.

For twenty minutes I sat there and then Alloa came out again. For a second as he walked past me, our eyes met and I saw that he knew me. His eyes widened a little but he didn't stop. In two more seconds he was out of the front door and gone.

I picked up the telephone book and called Lord Alloa's number. 'Is Lord Alloa at home?' I asked.

'He came in half an hour ago, not feeling well, and has gone straight to bed,' was the answer.

There was not a minute to lose: I walked straight into the room where the other men were still in their meeting. Five surprised faces looked up: Drew, Winstanley, Whittaker, the French defence chief Royer and Sir Walter, who did not look pleased to see me.

'This is Mr Hannay, gentlemen,' he said. 'I have spoken to you about him. I'm afraid, Hannay, that this visit is most unwelcome.'

'We shall see, sir,' I answered quietly. 'Tell me, who left this room two minutes ago?'

'Lord Alloa,' Sir Walter answered, still very angry.

'No, it was not,' I cried. 'It was someone who looked just like him but it was not Lord Alloa. I've just telephoned his home and he's been there for the last half hour. He's already in bed.'

'Who – who –?' someone shouted.

Then Lord Alloa came out again. As he walked past me, our eyes met and I saw that he knew me. His eyes widened a little but he didn't stop.

'The Black Stone,' I said softly and sat down in the empty chair where our enemy was sitting only a few minutes before. Five gentlemen with very frightened faces looked at me across the table.

Chapter Nine

THE THIRTY-NINE STEPS

It took some time for everyone in the room to understand that the man they thought was Lord Alloa was really a different person. But then Sir Walter went to telephone the real Lord Alloa and they realized that my story was quite true.

'But how could he remember all those facts and numbers?' asked the General.

'There are people who remember things perfectly – photographically,' said the Frenchman. 'They can teach themselves to do it.'

'Can we change the plans?' asked Sir Walter. Everyone agreed that to do this quickly was too difficult.

'We must find these people and stop them from getting back to Germany,' Royer said. 'It's the only way. I talked freely about my government's defence plans also, while he was here. That information is just what our enemies want. I know their ways: they will not try to send the information by post because they always prefer to give it in person. So they are still somewhere in this country.'

Suddenly I had a wonderful idea. 'Where's Scudder's notebook?' I asked. Sir Walter went to a desk and brought it. I found the right page.

'"The thirty-nine steps,"' I read. '"Thirty-nine steps – I counted them – high water 10.17 p.m." That's how they're going to get away and tomorrow was the day they planned! They'll escape by sea tomorrow evening at a place with thirty-nine steps. How can we find a book with the times of the **tides**?'

'Let's ask the Navy Office,' said Sir Walter. The rest of us got into two cars, while he went to see MacGillivray at Scotland Yard. The Navy Office gave us the Tide Book but there were about fifty places where the high tide was at 10.17 p.m.

On the way back to Sir Walter's house, I thought some more. Why was the high tide so important? I guessed that the boat they planned to use was a small one and the place was not an ordinary **port**. It was also clear that they were not planning to leave from Scotland or some other part of the country far away from London. This meant that we had to look for a place on the open coast where there were thirty-nine steps going down to the sea and where the high tide next day was at 10.17 p.m.

When we were back at Queen Anne's Gate with the Tide Book, MacGillivray joined us. His men were already watching for our three enemies at all the ports and airports in the country. By now I was the one heading this group of top army, navy and Foreign Office men but no one seemed to find that strange. I turned to Whittaker. 'What we want now is someone who knows every bit of the South-East coast,' I said.

'I think I know just the right person,' Whittaker answered. 'He was a coastguard for forty years or more. Now he lives in Clapham.' A car went for the man and at one in the morning he came in.

'What we're looking for is a place on the South or East

51

'What we're looking for is a place with high ground and steps going down to the sea.'

coast with high ground and steps going down to the sea,' I explained, pointing to a map.

He showed us a place in Norfolk – Brattlesham – but we all agreed it was too far north. 'Well, there's the Ruff,' he said.

'What's that?' I asked.

'It's a big headland near Bradgate in Kent, with houses at the top which all have stairs going down to the beach.'

This seemed promising. I quickly looked up the Book of Tides: '"Bradgate, 15th June: high tide 10.27 p.m." That's it!' I cried. 'How can we find out the tide times at the Ruff?'

'I know that bit of the coast well,' the old man said. 'It's ten minutes earlier than at Bradgate.'

I closed the book and looked at the watching faces. 'If one of those stairs has thirty nine steps, then we have the answer, gentlemen,' I said. 'Sir Walter, please let me borrow your car and a good road map. I need Mr MacGillivray's help for ten minutes, so we can get something ready for to-morrow.'

There was a short silence. Then General Royer spoke for all the men there. 'I, for one, am happy to leave this matter in Mr Hannay's hands.'

By half past three in the morning, I was flying past the fields of Kent in Sir Walter's car, with MacGillivray's best man sitting next to me.

Chapter Ten

THE MEETING BY THE SEA

The morning of the 15th of June found me at Bradgate, looking out at a calm sea. A small warship lay about two miles out and Scaife, the Scotland Yard detective, told me its name. I phoned Sir Walter with this information.

After breakfast we started out for the Ruff. I didn't want anyone to see me, so I left Scaife to walk along the empty beach, looking at the stairs and counting the steps. When I saw him coming back, my heart was in my mouth. Was my guess right?

'Thirty-four, thirty-five, thirty-nine, forty-two, forty-seven,' he read out. I jumped up and nearly shouted out.

We hurried back to Bradgate and telephoned MacGillivray at Scotland Yard. I wanted six men, I told him. Then Scaife went off to look at the house at the top of the thirty-nine steps. On his return, I learned that it was called Trafalgar Lodge and belonged to an old gentleman called Appleton. He didn't live there all the time but he was there now. Scaife went round to the back door and talked to the cook, hoping to find out more, but she soon shut the door in his face. It seemed that she knew nothing.

I borrowed Scaife's field glasses and had a good look at the house. It was an ordinary square-built house, with quite a big garden, where you could play tennis, and with the usual seaside flowers. I saw someone leave the house and walk along the top of the headland. Through my glasses, I saw that he was an old man with white trousers, a blue jacket and a sun hat. He was carrying fieldglasses and a newspaper and soon he sat down to read it. From time to time he put down his paper and looked out to sea through the glasses, watching the warship for several minutes. After half an hour he got up and went back to the house for lunch, so I went off to Bradgate for mine. But I was still unsure. Was the old man the same as the one who took me prisoner? It was difficult to say.

Then after lunch, I saw what I was hoping for. A

sailing-boat of about 150 tons came up from the south and stopped opposite the Ruff. It seemed to be one of ours. Scaife and I went down to the sea and took out a boat for an afternoon's fishing. It was a warm, still afternoon and between us we caught plenty of fish. We could see Trafalgar Lodge clearly from quite far away. About four o'clock I asked the boatman to take us round the sailing-boat, which lay resting on the water like a beautiful white bird, ready to fly away at any minute.

The boat was named the Ariadne. I called out to one of the sailors and both he and the others who answered were clearly British from the way they spoke. Then an officer appeared and he, too, spoke to us in very good English: but I knew from the cut of his clothes and his close-shaven head that he was a foreigner.

This made me feel a little better but there were still many questions to answer. As we went back into Bradgate, I asked myself how much the Germans knew about Scudder and his information. What if they changed their plans? I decided to go back to Trafalgar Lodge and watch what was happening. This time two men were playing tennis: one was the old man and the other was younger but quite large. There was a lot of shouting and laughing over the game. They looked just like two city gentlemen on holiday. Were they really Scudder's killers?

After some time another young man arrived on a bicycle, carrying a sports bag. All three went into the house. Were they playing a part? If so, they were doing it perfectly. They looked to me like real Englishmen. And yet there were three of them: one old man, one large one, and one thin and dark; and Scudder's information – the date, the thirty-nine steps – all seemed to be right.

55

I went back and found Scaife and we agreed where to place his men. It was almost eight o'clock but I didn't want any supper. I went for a walk instead. I could see the lights come on in the Ariadne and on the warship away to the south. The whole place seemed so quiet and ordinary that I had to make myself return to Trafalgar Lodge.

I went up to the door and asked for Mr Appleton. Without thinking, I gave my real name. A woman asked me to wait in the sitting-room, which had old school photographs on the walls, but I could hear voices from the dining-room, so I walked straight in there. The old man was in evening dress, sitting at the head of the table. The other two – the fat one and the thin dark one – were on either side, the first also in evening dress and the second wearing an ordinary suit and an old school tie. Hiding my fears, I pulled up a chair and sat down.

'I think we have met before,' I said, 'and I guess you know my business.'

The light in the room was low but all three faces, as far as I could see, showed great surprise.

'Perhaps,' answered the old man, 'but I can't remember. Kindly tell me what your business is.'

'Well, then,' I said, 'I've come to tell you that your little game is finished. I'm here to arrest you three gentlemen.'

'Arrest us?' said the old man, looking still more surprised. 'Good God! What for?'

'For the murder of Franklin P. Scudder in London on the 23rd of last month.'

'I've never heard the name before,' said the old man, un-believing.

One of the others now spoke. 'That was the Portland Place murder. I read about it. Good God, you must be mad, sir! Where do you come from?'

'I think, sir, you can see that you have made a mistake.'

'Scotland Yard,' I answered.

For a minute there was silence. The old man looked down at his plate, his fingers playing with a piece of bread.

'Don't worry, father,' said the fat younger man. 'It's all a stupid mistake. We all know that I was out of the country on the 23rd of May and Bob here was in hospital. You were in London on that day but you can easily explain what you were doing.'

'Of course,' said the old man. 'It was the day after Agatha's wedding. I remember now I had lunch with Charlie Symonds and went on to a dinner in the City.'

'I think, sir, you can see that you have made a mistake,' the fat one said to me politely.

57

'I'm beginning to find it all quite amusing,' said the old man with a smile. 'What a story to tell my friends!'

By now my heart was in my boots and my first idea was to say I was sorry and leave at once. But I had to make quite sure. It didn't really matter if I made a fool of myself. To cover my confusion, I got up, switched on the ceiling lights and looked hard at the three faces: one old and hairless, one fat, one dark-eyed and thin. But in no other way did they seem like the men who took me prisoner in Scotland.

'Let's play a game of cards,' said the fat young man. 'It will give Mr Hannay time to think things over. Will you play, sir?'

So there we sat playing cards together. It was like a bad dream. The window was open and the moon threw a silvery light on the sea below. I played very badly. This pleased them greatly, I could see. I kept looking at their faces but they showed me nothing. These people not only looked different: they *were* different.

The clock on the wall showed ten o'clock. Then a small thing caught my eye: something very ordinary.

The old man put down his hand to take a cigar. He didn't pick it up at once but let his hand rest on his knee, the fingers moving like someone playing the piano. I nearly missed it but I didn't. It was the movement I remembered from the house in Scotland, when I stood before him with the guns of his men at my back. Suddenly I knew. They were the same men. The young dark one was the killer: now I could see it in his face. The fat one's face was like rubber. He was probably the 'Lord Alloa' of the night before. Scudder said that he spoke with a lisp, perhaps to seem more frightening. But the old man was their chief – cold, hard, with a perfectly shaped intelligence. I went on playing, but with hate in my heart now.

The clock showed nearly half past ten.

The young man jumped through the window and ran towards the stairs down to the sea.

'Hey, Bob! Look at the time!' said the old man. 'You have to catch your train back to London.'

'I'm afraid that will not be possible,' I said.

'But I must go,' the dark-haired man said. 'I'll give you my address, if you like.'

'No,' I said. 'You're staying here.'

'My son and I will be here,' said the old man quickly. 'Surely that is enough for you, Mr Hannay.' And as he spoke, I saw the eyelids come down and cover his eyes in the way that frightened me so much once before.

I blew my whistle.

Immediately the lights went out. A pair of strong arms held me, feeling my pockets for a gun.

'Quick, Franz,' a voice cried in German. 'Get to the boat!' At the same time I saw two policemen running across the grass outside the window.

The young dark man jumped through the window and ran towards the stairs down to the sea. Inside, the room was suddenly full of people, as I fought with the old man. But my eyes were on Franz as he flew down the steps, locking the door to them behind him.

The old man broke free. 'He's safe!' he shouted. 'You cannot follow him now. The Black Stone has won!' His eyes burned, not just with hate for his enemies but with love for his country; in his way, he too was doing what he believed in, just like us.

But I had the last word. 'I hope Franz will be proud of himself,' I said calmly. 'For the last hour the Ariadne has been in our hands.'

Seven weeks later, as the world knows, Europe was at war. I went into the army in the first week; but I think my best work was already over before the war began.

60

EXERCISES

Vocabulary Work

Look back at the 'Dictionary Words' in this story. Make sure that you know the meaning of each word. Write sentences with the words in these groups:

    a arrest/gentleman/eyelids

    b engineer/tide/port

    c fact/tobacco/life

    d government/powers/political

    e defence/code/explosive

    f piano/whistling/torch

Comprehension

Chapters 1–2

1 Answer these questions.

    a What is Hannay's first name?

    b An old soldier cleans Hannay's rooms. What is his name?

    c Scudder talked about a Black ... What?

    d Hannay put on this man's flat blue hat and white coat. Whose?

    e Scudder did some writing for a newspaper in this city. Which city?

    f Where did Scudder come from in America?

Chapters 3–5

2 Here are four of the people Hannay meets in these chapters:

    Sir Harry   a drunk old man and his sheepdog   Marmaduke Jopley Sandy Turnbull

    a Which one does he meet first?

    b Which one does he meet last?

    c Where does he meet all these people?

Chapters 6–8

3 Are these sentences true ($\checkmark$) or not true ($\times$)?

  a The man with no hair moved his fingers like a piano-player.

  b Hannay found explosives in a locked cupboard.

  c Hannay drove Sir Walter to his house at Queen Mary's Gate.

  d Hannay had lunch at the Ritz Hotel.

Chapters 9–10

4 In these chapters, who:

  a told Hannay about the Ruff?

  b let Hannay borrow his car and a good road map?

  c borrowed Scaite's field glasses?

5 Answer these questions about the whole story.

  a Why was the name 'Julia Czechenyi' important in this story?

  b Who did Hannay say he was when his enemies caught him in the old farmhouse?

  c Which two words told Sir Walter who Hannay was?

  d Who saw Hannay again in a London street and tried to arrest him?

  e What did the words 'thirty-nine steps' mean?

Discussion

1 At the beginning of the story, Hannay is waiting for something exciting to happen. Some people like exciting things to do (mountains to climb, boats to take round the world). Can you think of any famous people like this?

2 Do you think Hannay always does the right thing? Would you sometimes do things differently if you were in his place?

Writing

1 a Look at the picture of Richard Hannay on page 14. Write two or three sentences about his clothes.

  b Look at the picture of him on page 34. Write two or three sentences about his clothes in this picture.

2 *You* are the milkman in Chapter 2. You meet Hannay and he borrows your hat and white coat; you find Scudder; you are arrested and then you are free again. Write about 200 words telling the story of your day.

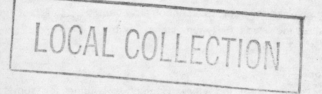